A Christmas Carol Revisited

Phil Rowlands

A Christmas Carol Revisited

Copyright © 2012 Phil Rowlands

All rights reserved.

ISBN: 1480075582
ISBN-13: **978-1480075580**

A Christmas Carol Revisited

DEDICATION

A Humble Tribute To A Great Man And Social Commentator

Charles Dickens

1812 – 1870

A Christmas Carol Revisited

CONTENTS

1 PART 1: Christmas Eve 5.15 p.m. Pg 8

2 PART 2: Christmas Eve 6.00 p.m. Pg 20

3 PART 3: Christmas Eve: Later Pg 42

4 PART 4: The Conclusion Pg 54

A Christmas Carol Revisited

ACKNOWLEDGMENTS

With special thanks to Family and Friends for their constant encouragement.
"Praise is like sunlight to the human spirit: we cannot flower and grow without it."
Jess Lair

PART 1: CHRISTMAS EVE 5.15 P.M.

Christmas Eve 5.15 p.m.

Through tinted windows Ebenezer Clinton Scrooge III watched the bustling side-walk crowds slip silently into the waiting night like shadowy grey wraiths spirited away on a bitter December wind. The gaudy festive lights served only to emphasize their desperate anonymity. Scrooge leaned back into the plush leather upholstery of the limousine, comforted by the fact he no longer needed to mingle with the madding crowd. It was as the car slowed at the intersection of 52nd Street he first thought he saw *'the face'*.

Someone was standing on the side-walk staring directly at him, which was actually impossible because from the outside the windows presented an impenetrable black veil. *Someone* the bubbling froth of humanity flowed around like water in a rushing stream as it breaks over an ancient immovable stone. *Someone* with eyes exactly like...no, that simply could not be! For an instant the chill night air embraced him rendering impotent the luxurious heated interior of the imported Bentley.

He leaned forward striking his face sharply against the glass in a futile attempt to confirm or more likely disprove his initial impression. The figure was no longer there. Ahead the congestion eased slightly and the limousine moved on with menacing grace through the swarming rush-hour traffic. A simple trick of the light that was all. Besides, they say everyone has a double but there had been no mistaking the irascible gleam that always alerted Scrooge to the fact his old partner and adversary had gauged exactly the subtle machinations of his devious mind.

Strange, it was a sensation that momentarily overwhelmed him with nostalgia. He was not a sentimental man, far from it, but he missed the challenge of an equal. In the days and years following *'the accident'* there had been no one of sufficient intellect and force of character to hinder Scrooge's ruthless march to power. Control the media and you control the masses. He smiled to think that while the world was to all intents and purposes unaware of his existence he could at will reach inside the minds of men and plant seeds that took root grew and bore fruit, very profitable fruit indeed.

That is what had caused the rift and with each passing day it widened until a yawning chasm opened between them that nothing on this earth could bridge. It was not that either man was opposed to employing manipulation as a perfectly acceptable means of influencing the thoughts and opinions of the vast global audience the company had amassed via its satellite, television and media empire. Mind control through such channels as subliminal messaging was a universally accepted marketing method employed by all the major corporations whether you wanted someone to buy a particular brand of toilet roll or plunge a nation into war.

'Plunge a nation into war!'

Beads of perspiration began to merge and trickle in tiny rivulets down Scrooge's brow. As he dabbed at them the source of his sudden unease broke through the surface of his consciousness like a drowning man's last desperate bid for air. They were words that had once been uttered accusingly in his direction with a vehemence that had momentarily reduced him to silence. Words that had severed the final frayed bond of friendship forever. Jake's words.

"It's almost Time Ebenezer."

The sudden interruption of his reverie by a disembodied voice on the car's internal intercom startled him. He pressed a button and opened communication with Grainger, his Chauffeur.

"What did you say Grainger?" Although even as he spoke he knew the answer. Grainger would not dare to be so familiar. It had not been Grainger's voice he had heard.

"Nothing Sir, at least not just then, but I have been trying to speak with you for the last ten minutes. The intercom must be playing up."

"It would be easier to waken the dead!"

"Pardon!" Scrooge swallowed hard. His throat had become unusually constricted.

"I said the intercom must be playing up, sir. Seems as if we have a few gremlins in our systems tonight. Apparently the lift to your private car park is jammed. We'll have to stop outside and use the main entrance."

"With the common herd!"

That voice again. Not Grainger's but another he knew all too well.

Leaning forward he peered over Grainger's unsuspecting shoulders into the mirror above his chauffeur's head. Dark brown eyes stared back at him, eyes that could not be Grainger's because his were blue. The eyes blinked and they were blue again. Scrooge produced a large silken handkerchief and began to mop his brow. It was oppressively warm; perhaps gremlins had also managed to disrupt the air conditioning.

His head began to throb. Whether as a direct consequence of having struck it against the strengthened glass or the sudden unwelcome revelation that he did not want Grainger to turn around because he was no longer certain the presence seated directly in front of him was Grainger. This was absurd!

The car pulled up in front of the monstrous edifice that Scrooge recognized at once as home. He exhaled and the tension flooded from him. Get a grip! What an earth had come over him. A vaguely familiar face in the crowd and his imagination had gone off on one Big Time, to quote the vernacular, something he normally avoided at all cost. He sank back into the welcoming folds of the padded interior as the car slowed gently to a stop. Though normally impervious to the pressures that oppress powerful men he had to confess to himself that the recent clandestine 'arrangement' made with certain shadowy emissaries of State had provoked in him the first spasms of anxiety experienced since…well, a long time. After Watergate no-one could be considered immune and what if this new 'venture' was a bridge too far? Too late now, the dye had been cast; besides the potential pay-off was immense.

"Here we are sir."

"Final Destination."

The words jolted Scrooge back into the present scattering his thoughts like a flock of startled crows. 'Final Destination', the phrase evoked morbid images of hapless teenagers meeting untimely ends in a variety of ingenious and gruesome ways. Not that he was particularly averse to the idea of such a fate befalling a sizeable portion of the youthful population. What use were most of them anyway? Drugs and sex seemed to be the only activities they indulged in with any enthusiasm. The language they spoke was by and large totally incomprehensible and unless they enlisted in the armed forces, where their energies could be channeled and directed to more constructive purposes, Scrooge saw little to justify their aimless existence.

Grainger opened the driver's door and Scrooge watched his large bulk disappear onto the side-walk with a growing apprehension that he was unable to exorcise. Normally Grainger's presence was a source of reassurance, offering protection and exuding intimidation in equal measure. No Caesar felt more secure surrounded by his Praetorian Guard than did Scrooge with the massive figure of Grainger at his side. But not today. An ominous sense of foreboding seeped like fog into the interior of the limousine and he was a child again hiding under his bed while the familiar dread footfalls ascended the staircase before halting deliberately outside his bedroom door. The silence was always the worst holding within itself all the pregnant possibilities of a child's fear.

Silhouetted against the smoked glass Grainger appeared somehow much smaller and infinitely more menacing. Obeying a primal instinct Scrooge moved hastily to secure the internal lock just as a hand attempted to open the door from the outside.

How many times had Grainger performed this same procedure shielding his master from any possible unwanted media attention with his huge frame as Scrooge emerged warily from his black cocoon? Thousands probably. But today was different and the door was already being pulled open from the outside with irresistible force. There was no bed to cower under so he eased himself out into the grey December twilight.

No one was there. Where was Grainger and if he hadn't opened the door then who had? Scrooge remained with his back to the limousine reluctant to abandon the potential sanctuary it might yet offer. Then he saw Grainger. He was about 20 yards away seemingly engaged in a one-sided wrestling match with some unfortunate individual who now lay pinned to the floor but obviously not yet fully subdued. Scrooge surveyed the immediate area with mounting alarm. Could there be more than one assailant? He was aware that the latest project he had agreed to pursue was not without risk but had not anticipated that risk being of a physical nature. Certainly not as crude as an assault on the street in broad daylight. And where was Security? Surely they would have been waiting for him to arrive once they knew the private lift had developed a fault. Something was very wrong.

Prevarication was not one of Scrooge's vices and having assessed the situation he swiftly determined a course of action. Taking refuge in the limousine, although tempting, was not a viable option. Determined individuals bold enough to perpetrate an assault on the very steps of the citadel of his personal empire would not be deterred by a locked door. Obviously *'they'* had succeeded in jamming communications between the limousine and his supposedly secure communication channel at *'Interstellar Inc.'* which would account for the absence of Security and senior members of staff. It would also indicate that whoever had planned this had access to some very serious hardware indeed.

There were no signs of angels or demons on the marble steps that rose like Jacob's ladder from the frozen side-walk. He was alone and vulnerable waiting for darkness to fall and the call of the Bogeyman. To his left Grainger appeared to have the situation completely under control but why was he marching the unfortunate individual towards Scrooge and not in the opposite direction? Wasn't Caesar murdered by those he thought most loyal to him? Shadowy figures were beginning to descend the marble steps towards them. Security had obviously gotten their act together at last. He glanced at Grainger who had stopped a few feet away with the unfortunate individual securely and painfully in his grip. Scrooge decided to err on the side of discretion. Leaving the individual in the tender care of Grainger he turned to ascend the steps of his citadel.

Two steps up he paused. There was something not quite right. The figures on the steps were still moving towards him but very slowly. In fact they were moving in step, keeping pace with each other, like mourners he had once watched following a funeral cortège. He remembered it as if it were yesterday. It had been Jacob's funeral. He stepped back.

Grainger was still standing several feet away holding a scruffy individual who had now stopped struggling and succumbed to the inevitable. His face was almost hidden beneath long greasy strands of what Scrooge determined must have once been blonde hair. His beard was matted and hid what appeared to be a mass of ugly scarring that tugged the skin around his eye down towards his disfigured cheek. Scrooge observed with some distaste that he was missing a left forearm.

He smiled, this was no hired assassin sent on a mission to destroy only a common beggar chancing his arm, or what remained of it. A diseased symptom of the times. New York was infested with such hopeless individuals seeking solace and oblivion in alcohol or drugs, authors of their own destruction, and as such deserving of no sympathy or special favors. Still they never usually surfaced in this district preferring instead to haunt the more stagnant cess-pits of the city. Perhaps the fact it was Christmas Eve had emboldened this particular specimen into venturing further afield in the false hope that honest citizens would be more inclined to lunatic displays of charity many being so imbued with festive spirits they would carelessly part with their hard earned dollars.

The man had the audacity to stare brazenly at Scrooge as though faced with an equal. Why hadn't Grainger simply sent him packing? Attuned by long years of service to his master's thought's Grainger responded quickly.

"I would have sent him on his way Sir, but he says he knows you."

"Have you completely lost it man? Does he look remotely like someone who mixes in the same social circles?"

But even as he uttered the words awareness rose like an unsettling mist from some dark subterranean reservoir of his mind that somewhere in a previous existence he had crossed paths with this wretched creature. He extinguished the thought as easily as a lit candle.

Suddenly conscious of his plight the beggar averted his eyes, now dark and heavy as though their light too had dimmed.

"I thought..."

"I know what you thought." Scrooge's every word dripped with contempt, "The same your sort always thinks."

To his astonishment the creature lifted its gaze and eyes no longer cowed held Scrooges scornful gaze until it was he who almost felt compelled to look away.

"Merry Christmas." The stranger spoke the words with a slow deliberation as though he sat in judgment and pronounced sentence on a man found guilty of a heinous crime.

Anger surged through Scrooge robbing him of speech and forcing his hands into tightly clenched fists. He stepped forward one hand raised above his head poised to strike the blow his impotent tongue was incapable of delivering.

"Leave this to us Sir."

Large ominous shapes brushed past Scrooge and took hold of the unfortunate individual who had dared carry the pungent odor of failure and despair to the very steps of this towering capitalist monument they had been chosen to protect. Security had arrived and not before time. In truth, Scrooge was mightily relieved, physical violence had never been his forte and the thought of actual contact with that foul individual made his skin crawl. Instead he watched with quiet satisfaction as the lowlife was manhandled down the side-walk before being sent sprawling on his way.

Had he bothered to watch the young man struggle painfully to his feet he might have been somewhat surprised by the sad shake of the head as his eyes followed Scrooge's regal ascent up the marble staircase. By the time Scrooge had reached the summit he had already disappeared into the encroaching darkness.

Security had cleared the lobby. A Christmas tree adorned with twinkling lights and red bows enjoyed its transient celebrity status amid the opulent surroundings. The day after tomorrow, stripped of its baubles, it would be cast aside as trash as though it had never been. With a dismissive gesture he waved Security away and crossed the deserted lobby alone. This was his domain he needed no protection and the sound of his footfalls reverberating off the marble floor comforted him. In truth the encounter with the vagrant had unsettled him as had the journey through the city's crowded streets. He had fallen asleep and experienced an unusually vivid dream that was all. Now he was almost home.

His private lift was situated at the end of a corridor that could only be accessed via a concealed alcove. Very few people were even aware of its existence and that was the primary reason the sight of a young child standing by the steel doors stopped Scrooge dead in his tracks. The girl had her back to him. Long auburn hair flowed over the back of her pink party dress. Scrooge estimated her to be about nine or ten years old. Had one of the staff organized a party without his knowledge? If so there would be repercussions.

"Children and business don't mix."

A familiar voice startled him and he half turned to see who had taken the liberty of following him. Probably the same idiot who had brought the child into the building in the first place. Scrooge blinked, then rubbed his eyes as though attempting to clear away a persistent fog that obscured his vision. It made no difference, the corridor behind him was empty, not a soul in sight. He was obviously sickening for something. What he needed was a neat brandy. The sooner he got to his suite the better.

The child was still standing by the lift but now she was staring straight at Scrooge through sapphire blue eyes that reminded him of the feral Persian cat that had once slipped into the building unobserved until he had come across one of the cleaners feeding it scraps. That had been the end of the cat, and the cleaner. He opened his lips to demand an explanation for her presence but he found his lips were dry and his tongue clove to the roof of his mouth. As he stood and watched the elevator doors opened and she slipped inside. This was intolerable.

Scrooge sprinted towards the lift just in time to hold and open the doors. He almost tumbled inside. Perspiration trickled down his forehead stinging his eyes. His breath came in short, heavy gasps. There would be a reckoning once he discovered who the girl's father was. Bringing a child to work and allowing it the freedom to run wild through his private areas. The lift was empty. At first he refused to believe the evidence of his own eyes. He closed them, counted to three and opened them again but the child was gone. His collar was unusually tight, constricting his breathing. He loosened his tie and slumped back against the cold hard steel. His blurred image reflected upon the opposite side of the elevator also loosened its tie but there was one difference. Someone stood beside his reflection, looking up intently into his face.

A child with auburn hair. The reflection was indistinct as though he was viewing the scene through misted glass yet he thought her face expressed a deep sadness and he himself was its source.

The doors opened and the familiar glow of his personal reception foyer beckoned him home.

"Good evening Sir. Is something the matter?"

Eva Perry, his personal secretary, stood outside the lift a look of professional concern on her face but Scrooge did not notice her expression. He was staring into the empty confines of the elevator. Miss Perry moved forward and did the same.

"Have you lost something?"

"What?"

With difficulty Scrooge tore his gaze away from the reflection of the child who now stood alone her face still turned towards him. "Would you mind taking a look inside?

Miss Perry."

She glanced at her employer as she stepped into the lift.

"Well?"

The urgency his voice conveyed could only mean that something of great significance was missing.

"What exactly am I looking for Sir?"

"You don't see her?"

"See whom? You were the only person in the lift Mr. Scrooge. "

"A child." A little girl with auburn hair. Wandering around unaccompanied."

"No one is allowed on this level without your express permission and security clearance."

Was it possible he had been drinking this early? She knew his habits intimately; he was a man of strict routines and never took a drink before six at the earliest. Still this was the festive season and folk were more likely to drop their guard and over indulge at this time of year than any other. No, this was Scrooge after all, he was less likely to over indulge at Christmas than any man alive.

"I am fully aware I was the only person in the lift Miss Perry. I just wondered if you had seen the child I described or some evidence that she had been inside the elevator. "

"No, no children of any persuasion Sir."

He was lying, of that she was certain, but why?

Scrooge watched the elevator doors close. The child stood there watching him, trapped like a body floating beneath the surface of a shimmering metallic pool, until the doors closed completely and she was gone forever.

"There is someone waiting to see you though. He's been waiting quite some time…

A corpulent individual was seated in large chair in the foyer. He stood when Scrooge exited the lift. The movement had caught his eye.

"Then he'll have to wait a little longer. Make sure I'm not disturbed for at least an hour."

The figure slumped back down assuming a distinctly dejected posture.

Without even acknowledging the individual's presence Scrooge crossed the foyer and entered his private quarters. The solid mahogany doors closed behind him with a reassuringly solid thud.

2 CHRISTMAS EVE 6.00 P.M.

Christmas Eve 6.00 p.m.

Tatters of desperate fog clung to the tower buildings stubbornly resisting the freezing tug of the implacable wind. Like the hulks of submerged haunted wrecks emerging from some anonymous watery grave the dark outline of the city took shape and grew. Wisps of grey fog drifted mournfully past the windows of the monolith that seemed almost to push and elbow its way above the mass of surrounding tower blocks as though the very elements themselves shrank back from contact with the cold indifferent stone.

Scrooge gazed out of the window. Somewhere below, the river flowed blacker than the Styx through the city's dark heart into the eternal depths of the poisoned oceans. But Scrooge's eyes were fixed upon another river. The unceasing flow of humanity condemned as surely to follow the course of existence to its inevitable conclusion as the river was compelled to flow into the embrace of the blind and restless sea.

Christmas held out hope that the journey was not in vain. That was one of the reasons he despised it. Christmas was for the weak, for sentimental fools who had never grasped that salvation in this world was something to be wrung forcefully from life's unwilling grip. Once the presents had been opened and the parties were over what was left apart from hangovers and a bigger overdraft? He smiled. He was above that now, had been for years. Just as detached and aloof as the gigantic reflection of himself superimposed on the vista upon which he cast such a scornful eye.

Scrooge blinked. Surely not! It was his imagination. Sentimentality was infectious but until now he had considered himself immune from that particular disease. Yet what else could explain it? He rubbed his eyes. Overwork, he had always worked hard, perhaps too hard. Maybe even he needed a rest. There was no doubting what he had seen. The reflection in the glass that had once been his own was undoubtedly that of Jake Marley, the very dead Jake Marley. Slowly he opened his eyes. Nothing, just his own reflection staring coldly back at him from above the city like some eternally lost and disembodied soul. Steady! This was most unlike him. He needed a drink, a stiff drink.

Scrooge turned abruptly away from the window and headed for the cocktail cabinet. Normally he never indulged except to toast a successful business deal or the demise, metaphorically or otherwise, of a competitor. After all business was war. There were winners and there were losers. Scrooge had always been a winner, no matter what it took. Sure there were casualties, that was the nature of war, and Jake Marley had been one of them. That however, had not been down to him. On that matter his hands were clean and his conscience clear. Jake and he had been partners. True Jake had always been a little soft but what had happened had nothing to do with Ebenezer Clinton Scrooge III. Then why was he troubled by an emotion that was so unfamiliar to him? Surely, this could not be guilt?

He poured himself a generous Scotch and sat down heavily on the chair at the head of the large polished rectangular boardroom table that over the years had become his personal domain. The contents of the glass he downed in one, catching his breath as the alcohol surged against the back of his throat. It was a long time since he'd felt the need to down a drink with such urgency. The last time was when the police had brought him the news about Jake.

Jake had never gone for the deal in the first place. The ensuing board meeting had been bitter and uncompromising. Scrooge had convinced the majority that the merger was in everyone's best interests, vital, in fact, to corporate survival. It had been his finest hour. Jake had provided stiff opposition but, as always, his argument was based on weakness, the main thrust being that rather than a merger the company was entering into a pact with Lucifer himself. You could almost smell the fire and brimstone. It was compelling stuff. Some of the Board had been spooked by Jake's lurid interpretation of the consequences. Admittedly there had been rumors, stories that their potential partners were not entirely what it seemed. Jake had gone so far as to suggest the company concerned was merely a front for certain powerful and unscrupulous government agencies. It was a dangerous moment. Jake Marley was not a man who could naturally claim the moral high ground in any argument, a fact Scrooge exploited ruthlessly. Scrooge reminded the Board that rejection of the merger on the grounds outlined by Jake would result in litigation. Serious litigation the company could not sustain. By the end of the meeting the deal was practically signed and sealed and the company firmly in Scrooges' grip.

Jake proved a sore loser muttering threats that involved private investigators and the Press. Nothing ever happened. Three weeks later Jake's car, complete with Jake, was fished out of the river. The coroner's verdict recorded 'death by misadventure' but the story circulated how high levels of alcohol had been found in Jake's blood. Just another drunk driver who this time got his just desserts. Only Scrooge and the rest of the Board knew that although Jake had many vices drink was no longer one of them. Excessive abuse in his younger days had devastated his liver. Jake was strictly tee-total, had been for years, though that was where his temperance ended.

Still, what was done was done. Jake was dead and corporate life must go on. The funeral had proved an embarrassment. Scrooge guessed it would when the family sent his flowers back suggesting he might need some when his time came. He had no choice but to attend as his absence would only have fuelled some of the more wildly speculative and lurid rumors regarding his involvement in Jake's death. Banquo must have felt more welcome at Macbeth's feast. Every time he glanced across Jake's widow's eyes burned accusingly at him like coals through black smoke.

A face stared up at him from the polished surface of the table. A hard face. A face fashioned down the long years on the anvil of power by the hungry hammer of greed. Deep, humorless lines marked ruthless paths into the very essence of his being. Cold blue eyes stared from the depths of the table like the dead empty eyes of a drowning man. Scrooge flinched. Wherever possible he avoided mirrors. Time had not been kind, or so he said. Truth was that Time had simply recorded faithfully the portrait of his life on the canvas of his face. He was about to turn his head when the image in the table winked at him and grinned.

The solid oak chair spilled backwards as Scrooge leapt from the lips of a bottomless pit that seemed suddenly to be opening wide before him. His calves throbbed from the violent impact but he could not avert his eyes held as they were by a terrible fascination. There could be no doubt; the reflection was that of Jake Marley. No mistaking the slightly lop-sided grin, the mischievous twinkle in those dark brown eyes and the compromising wink that always preceded some frivolous remark usually uttered at Scrooge's discomforted expense.

Nameless ice-cold insects crawled the length of his spine as the horror evolved and grew. He gazed not upon the polished mahogany expanse of table but on the liquid surface of an oily pool in whose depths the body of Jake Marley slowly sank. Jake Marley no longer winked, his eyes now black holes through which small fishes swam, his grin the skeletal grimace of a long dead cadaver. Yet even as Scrooge watched Jake's jaw bone moved as though trying to speak across the unbridgeable chasm that separates the living from the dead. Words formed and took shape inside Scrooge's head, words that bubbled upwards from some dark watery subterranean place.

"Tonight Ebenezer. Expect me tonight."

Other shapes drifted and floated around Jake Marley's receding form. Blue-black bloated bodies arms extended in desperate and futile attempts to break the surface, reach out towards Scrooge and drag him down to a dark and silent communion.

There were those he thought he recognized. Among them a sacked employee who had taken his own life because he lacked the backbone to find another job. They looked at him as Jake's widow had done. Enough was enough! Clenching his fist Scrooge smashed it down hard upon the table surface. It did not sink into unknown depths instead the shock of violent contact with an unresisting object reverberated painfully the length of his arm. His own face looked up at him unforgiving.

"Must have been a bad batch of Scotch." he muttered. "I'll sue the son of a bitch."

The prospect of suing someone partially restored Scrooge's good humor. Yet the boardroom table had become an alien and hostile object, a portal to dark worlds from which he shrunk, forbidding his fevered imagination to step across the beckoning threshold. Could objects be alien and hostile? Surely that was the realm of fantasy and science fiction and Scrooge was nothing if not pragmatic. Still, he needed to stretch his legs, move around, and get the blood to circulate oxygen to his brain.

He found himself back at the window. Sweat beaded his brow. Perhaps he was sickening for something. The thought comforted Scrooge. If he was going to be sick why not now? The festive season was a futile dissipation of Man's most precious commodity, Time. He despised the way it was squandered wantonly every year. How many people really enjoyed Christmas anyhow? The obligatory family get-togethers, the gifts nobody wanted the spoilt ungrateful brats quarrelsome and bored before the turkey had gone cold. When the bank statement arrived in the post come January the last Resolution evaporated before the chill winds of reality. Cynic he may be, but he always played the percentages and cynics were rarely disappointed when the dice finally came to rest.

He watched the silver twinkling tail-lights slither like slugs' trails through the tangled undergrowth of buildings. The windows of surrounding tower blocks were festooned with colored lights and baubles. He guessed many would return to work trying to forget the spectacles they made of themselves at the office party. How Jake had enjoyed office parties. He always drank too much and flirted outrageously but staff seemed to love him for it. You can stab a man in the back on Tuesday as long as you smiled and bought him a drink on Monday he won't even feel a thing. Scrooge had grudgingly acknowledged Jake's capacity for duplicity. He had style did Jake; you had to give him that. Look at him now for instance.

Look at him now! Scrooge blinked but there he was, Jake Marley, hovering outside the window 28 floors up, staring straight at Scrooge. The fever was getting hold or maybe the Scotch has been deliberately spiked with some kind of hallucinogenic drug. Scrooge placed his hands on the windows for support and bent over. He felt sick, was he going to faint? Scrooge despised weakness but this was not weakness, this was either a deliberate and malevolent act of sabotage or an inane practical joke inspired by the lunacy that appeared to afflict the herd instinct at Christmas and the New Year. Regardless of the motivation the consequence would be the same. Whoever was responsible was already dead in the water. Why did he have to think of water? An image of Jake sat at the seat of his submerged limousine, staring through hollow sightless eyes as the eager fishes gathered filled his mind. He jerked his head upwards and the image splintered and vanished.

His hands were still on the glass but now they pressed against another pair of hands. Black-green mottled hands, the hands of Jake Marley. It was not the diseased hands of a long dead man that forced a cry from Scrooge's lips but the sight of a face pressed against the glass like a naughty schoolboy attempting to disrupt a class from which he had been expelled. For a moment they were eyeball to eyeball, Scrooge could even see his terror reflected in the glassy stare before he stumbled backwards.

The corpse of Jake Marley pressed against the window and as it did so the glass yielded before its weight as though it were merely a thin film of plastic sheeting molding itself against the grim contours of the rotting cadaver. Instinctively Scrooge shielded his eyes in anticipation of the violent explosion of myriad shattered splinters of glass about to fly directly at him. Instead the window yielded like the surface of a still pool closing silently above the form of Jake Marley as it tumbled onto the boardroom floor at the feet of Ebenezer Clinton Scrooge III.

Scrooge watched as logic wrestled with fear for control of his mortal coil. He only had to remain calm and soon the effects of the drug would begin to diminish. Jake Marley rose unsteadily and as he did so droplets of water fell from his clothing forming an icy pool at his feet. A fedora was pulled down low so that eyes gleamed from the shadows of its face the lower portion of which was concealed behind a silk cravat but there was no mistaking that this was the remains of his late business partner. From deep within the silken folds a familiar voice gurgled a greeting.

"Aren't you going to offer your old friend a drink? Sorry I'm a bit late. You never could abide being kept waiting could you Ebenezer. Time was always too precious, your time in particular. Now, unlike you Ebenezer, I have all the time in this world and beyond."

The creature doffed the fedora and bowed. Mercifully, long strands of matted wet hair covered its face. "The late, very late Jake Marley at your service."

Scrooge was conscious of nails digging into the palms of his hand hard enough to draw blood.

"Maybe you figure I'm wet enough already." It placed the fedora firmly back into place and stood upright as it spoke,

The corpse laughed and logic fled leaving Scrooge at the mercy of a nameless terror. The dread sound was not of this world neither did it evoke an image of heavenly choirs but of darker unforgiving entities that had not come to announce Good Will to All Men and Scrooge in particular but tidings of an altogether different kind.

Scrooge squeezed his eyes shut tight and clasped clammy hands hard over his ears. Like a child hiding from the Bogeyman, if he denied his brain sensory stimulation his over heated imagination would cool down and the apparition return to the hidden depths of his subconscious from which it had risen unbidden. The stench that assailed his nostrils was pure corruption bottled and distilled in some charnel house in hell. Involuntarily he opened his eyes and gagging, covered his mouth with his hands.

"It's a long time since I brushed my teeth Ebenezer." Again the horrid laughter, echoes from another realm. "You have no objections if I sit down?"

The gruesome phantom crossed to the head of the table and sat down in The Chair.

"Never though I would achieve such an exalted position while you were still alive Ebenezer. I think you had better join me, you look like you've seen a ghost."

A sound that might have once been described as a chuckle bubbled to the surface. Jake Marley pointed to the chair at the bottom end of the table directly opposite him. Scrooge was conscious of a distinct weakening of the knees but he was damned if he was going to sit in *that* chair.

"Or maybe damned if you don't! There are much worse things than assuming the most lowly position in this life Ebenezer. Much worse! Sit!"

Whether it was the effects of the spiked drink or the shock of realizing that somehow the creature, rather the *illusion*, at the head of the table had read his thoughts, Scrooge complied with uncharacteristic meekness. Of course the thing could read his mind, it lived there. Whatever the next few moments brought he had only to remind himself that its tenancy was temporary. Once restored to his normal mental state the memory of Jake Marley would receive a permanent eviction order.

"Unless you see with your own eyes and touch with you own hands. You were ever the skeptic Ebenezer." The creature leaned forward. "You never listened to what I had to say. You never listened to anyone except Ebenezer Clinton Scrooge III."

"That's not true; I always valued your opinion." Careful, now he was beginning to argue with himself. He must hold tight to the fact that this thing was not real.

The creature leaned forward elbows on the table placing the tips of its gloved fingers against each other as though it were studying Scrooge. He imagined this was how a butterfly might feel before being impaled and exhibited for eternity in a glass tomb.

If there was one consolation it was that Jake's hands were now concealed in gloves. Wet black leather gloves that dripped a steady staccato beat on the surface of the table. Scrooge recognized the rhythm as that of his own pounding heart. The silence enveloped him like a weighted shroud. At length the creature spoke.

"You valued my opinion Ebenezer? How much?" It paused obviously awaiting a response.

There was no going back now. He had crossed an invisible intangible line, passed through a veil that separated reality from fantasy. Perhaps talking to oneself, even a self that assumed the form of a rotting corpse, was good therapy. Think positive, this needn't be a negative experience; Scrooge hated waste of any kind. There was obviously some unresolved inner conflict that needed to be worked out. At the end he would emerge refined and purged of contamination, the inevitable consequence of having to mingle with the common herd on a daily basis.

"How much?" This last question was delivered with a vehemence that Jake Marley had never displayed in this life. Scrooge shrank back as the creature rose from its chair and pointed an accusing corrupted finger in his direction.

"Well..." Scrooge was rarely lost for words but now they fled from his stuttering tongue like disturbed flies from a carcass.

"Thirty pieces of silver Ebenezer, the eternal price of betrayal." There was no longer anger in its voice but a sadness that reached out to Scrooge in a mournful embrace.

Scrooge struggled free of its cloying grip. This was intolerable!

"Betrayal?"

He had intended to sound outraged, to plant his standard on the high pinnacle of moral ground but was shaken at how his words stumbled feeble and defensive from his lips. "There was never any betrayal Jacob. It was business, pure and simple."

"Pure, pure, Ebenezer," Scrooge flinched before the creature's sarcasm. "You truly believe business can clothe your sinful nature with respectability." It shook its head solemnly. "Ebenezer, you have walked this earth naked for many years."

It was not a comforting thought. Certainly not good for the corporate image. If it was true why hadn't someone told him? Though it had taken a child to wise up the Emperor, he was afforded the privilege of an animated corpse who had apparently found religion since passing over to the Other Side. Steady, the phantom was obviously speaking metaphorically.

"Naked? I think not Jacob all my suits are genuine Armani, made to order and delivered personally."

His attempt at humor evoked no response. Humor had never been Scrooge's forte he was always unable to distinguish it from sarcasm. The all too tangible Shade of Jacob Marley shook its head mournfully and keeping its gaze transfixed on his former partner stood on 'The Chair' until he seemed to loom above Scrooge like some malevolent bird of prey, poised to strike.

Scrooge gazed up helplessly, resigned to his fate. This was one hell of a hallucination. Even as the thought slipped unbidden into his head Jacob Marley's ravaged features reassembled themselves into what Scrooge assumed was a grin that somehow managed to radiate amusement and malevolence in equal measure.

'Hell Ebenezer. You think this is hell? Look within yourself, the fires are even now consuming your shriveled soul."

This was the final straw. The only thing Scrooge felt consumed by right now was indignation. Propelled by a sudden surge of righteous anger he gripped the edge of the mahogany table and eye-balled the manifestation of his fevered imagination with a steely determination. But the words of defiance died a whimper on dry lips as he saw his twin selves reflected small and lost in the Stygian darkness of those orbs like plastic figures trapped forever in a glass globe where no flakes of snow would ever fall to light the eternal darkness.

The Being that had once been Jacob Marley stretched out a corrupted arm and pointed accusingly in his direction. Scrooge awaited the verdict without protest resigned now to the possibility that he may actually be teetering precariously over the precipice of madness.

"Ebenezer Clinton Scrooge III this night you are condemned to embrace your worst nightmare. Not once, not twice, but thrice before the clock strikes midnight…"

Despite the rising panic Scrooge could not suppress a growing irritation at the way Jake was beginning to sound more and more like an Aging Thespian hamming up his final appearance before ignominy consumed him forever.

Jake paused. Scrooge waited.

"Tonight, "Jake continued and Scrooge was almost persuaded he could detect a tone of amusement in the measured pronouncement of doom, "you will receive three invitations. "

What horrors awaited him? Before his mind's eye lurid visions of humiliation, pain and terror emerged like ephemeral shapes out of some primordial mist only to fragment and vanish as others more awful in their intensity took substance in their place.

Scrooge, mute with apprehension, awaited judgment.

But none came. Instead the creature slowly removed the silk cravat from the lower portion of his countenance.

"Because I just know how you love parties Ebenezer."

As soon as the last words were uttered the Jake-Thing pulled the cravat away completely and flung it at the trembling Scrooge. It fluttered unnoticed to the floor but what held Scrooge's undivided attention was the way Jake's jaw dropped open striking the mahogany surface of the boardroom table, several feet below, with a sickening thud. This was accompanied by an unearthly howling, that could have been laughter but whose source was something less human.

Scrooge screamed as he felt his fingers being forcibly prized by some external and malevolent force from his tenuous grip on reality. Below a yawning void beckoned. But it was not Scrooge who plunged headlong into the darkness for before he could avert his terrified eyes he witnessed the final confirmation of his temporary state of madness. Jacob Marley launched himself from the chair as though he were diving into the swimming pool he once loved to cavort in with his various lady friends back in his old Malibu mansion. The polished surface yielded before him and closed above him and Jacob Marley was gone. Gone? He was never really here!

A sudden hammering on the boardroom door reverberated through Scrooge's tense frame like an electric current. No, it was not possible. Slowly the door swung open. Only the solid mass of mahogany kept him from falling.

"Are you all right Sir?"

Suppressing an almost irresistible desire to whoop with relief Scrooge stoically held his emotions in check and merely nodded unable to trust himself to speak. Thank God, normality had returned.

You look rather pale. "Miss Perry, his personal secretary, did not normally inquire about his health, or anyone else's if the truth be told, so he guessed tonight's 'experience' had left a visible impression. "Only there's someone who'd like to speak with you if it's convenient." Mistaking her employer's silence as a sign of displeasure she added with uncharacteristic charity. "He's been waiting a long time and it is Christmas Eve."

"How long has he been waiting?" His eyelid began to twitch. That hadn't happened since 8th Grade. When would this nightmare end?

"He should have left about an hour ago Sir. Are you sure you don't want a glass of water or something? You look like you've..."

"No!" The vehemence in his voice even startled Scrooge. Miss Perry took a step backwards onto safer ground. "Just show him in. Then you can go Miss Perry."

"Very well Sir and Merry Christmas." She waited obviously anticipating some kind of response.

"What? Yes, you also Miss Perry."

Scrooge watched her back away her eyes betraying alarm and relief in equal measure. Muffled voices sounded outside followed by a tentative rap on the door.

"Come!"

Scrooge hoped the anxiety he felt rise like flood waters had not yet reached his voice. The door opened slightly and an overweight middle aged nondescript individual squeezed his way into the boardroom wearing an ingratiating smile that Scrooge found instantly offensive.

"Well?"

Scrooge was relieved to recognize the man as an employee who worked somewhere in Accounts. Incredibly he thought he even recalled the person's name, Bobby Scratchitt or something very similar. Hadn't his brother died on Sept 11th? He vaguely remembered a memo from Miss Perry regarding a sympathy card. Given the circumstances it had been the politically correct thing to do so he had given her permission to go ahead on his behalf. He might even have actually signed it. The man was shifting uneasily from foot to foot. It wasn't helping Scrooge's frayed nerves already stretched to breaking point.

"Spit it out man, I don't have all night!"

"No Ebenezer Scrooge...you have Eternity."

Did Scratchitt, if it truly was Scratchitt, really utter those words or was it a dislodged fragment of his hallucinogenic ordeal. Maybe Scratchitt was the perpetrator. Nobody could possibly be as inoffensive as he looked. He took a tentative step towards his employee half expecting the rancid form of Jake Marley to burst through the meek veneer of Scratchitt like some hostile alien entity leaving the man's discarded skin in a crumpled heap on the floor.

Intimidated by his employer's aggressive maneuver Bob Cratchitt stepped back but not before Scrooge lurched forward thrusting a bony finger into his chest. This was not going according to plan. He seemed to have antagonized his boss even before opening his mouth. Yet the very act of physical contact appeared to have appeased Scrooge's more aggressive tendencies. An expression of what could only be called relief flooded his features. Had he been drinking? Maybe that's why he kept himself locked away in his suite like some latter day Howard Hughes.

"Well Scratchitt?"

For a fleeting moment Bob Cratchitt thought he detected a hint of a smile flickering across those thin lips. Then it was gone like a pale winter sun hidden behind a darkening storm cloud.

"Scratch what Mr. Scrooge, Sir?"

He was beginning to feel feeling distinctly uneasy about Scrooge's strange behavior and this last request had done nothing to alleviate his mounting apprehension. Mentally he began to calculate the distance to the door. If it came to a footrace he wasn't in the best of shape and the thought of having to turn his back on a violent alcoholic projected vivid images of wanton violence on the blank screen of his imagination like trailers for a Tarrantino movie.

Scrooge rubbed his eyes. A staccato throbbing at his temples warned him of an impending headache. What was the fool talking about?

"Just state your business Scratchitt..."he was about to add, "I have a home to go to." But that would have been a lie. Not that he subscribed to the peculiar moral reservations many weaker individuals held regarding the 'truth' as they perceived it. A lie was a useful tool, a formidable weapon in skilled and ruthless hands. It was just that this particular lie discomforted him. Truth was it caused him pain but he could not admit to such vulnerability, especially to himself.

"Cratchitt, sir, Bob Cratchitt. Not Scratchitt."

An immense wave of relief swept over Bob Cratchitt. Scrooge had not been requesting some kind of perverse physical contact he'd just mispronounced his name. Now they would both laugh at the misunderstanding and the tension would dissipate. He could make his request in a more conducive atmosphere. He might even leave on first name terms.

"Whatever! Is that it? We've got your name wrong on the payroll?"

Hope shriveled at Scrooge's feet like a cowed dog no longer able to please its master. Bob Cratchitt swallowed hard. It would be easy to back down. Too easy. It was something Bob Cratchitt had been practicing all his miserable failed life. But this was not about him.

Sir, my boy Timmy, he's real sick."

He'd promised himself he would not get emotional but an image of Timmy's wasted little body threatened to overwhelm his defenses and he swallowed hard.

Scrooge studied Cratchitt as he would the minute details of some long and complex business contract but the subtle nuances of human behavior were a closed book to him and always had been. Interpreting Bob Cratchitt's emotional turmoil as an indication he had concluded what he had come to say Scrooge gestured dismissively that the audience was over.

"Very well Scratchitt, I'll get Payroll to amend your details and I'm sorry to hear about your boy. Now shut the door behind you on your way out."

The guy had actually waited over an hour just because someone had spelt his name wrong in Payroll. Why was he still standing there? He glowered at Cratchitt but the man seemed to be in some sort of catatonic trance. Just as he decided that it would be a wise precaution to summon Security the man opened his mouth and spoke. The words appeared forced from Cratchitt's lips as though reluctant to expose themselves to the withering intensity of Scrooge's scrutiny.

"It's not my name. I need more time off. An extension of my Christmas holiday. I don't want to be paid or anything."

This evening was getting weirder and weirder. Scrooge was momentarily nonplussed. Had he heard correctly? Was the man really asking for a longer holiday?

But before he could respond Scratchitt spoke again and this time the effort seemed to drain him of all his vitality.

"This will probably be Timmy's last Christmas. I just want to spend more time with him while I can."

So that was his game. Playing the old sympathy card. Did the guy know who he was dealing with?

"Very well Scratchitt. Take an extra week."

Wait for it, Scrooge smiled inwardly, here comes the sting in the tail.

"But you lose your two weeks vacation in the summer. You know full well the New Year's our busiest time."

Masterstroke! Once word got passed around that Scratchitt had lost a week instead of gaining one no one else was likely to repeat an exercise so inevitably doomed to failure. Strange, why was Scratchitt smiling? Sure it was a weak smile, like a pale winter sun, but a smile none the less.

"Thank you Sir," he replied looking genuinely grateful. This guy could act. "I won't be needing another vacation this year."

What had he missed? Whatever angle Scratchitt was working Scrooge hadn't figured it out yet. But he would and when he did Scratchitt wouldn't know what hit him. He'd have this guy watched closely from now on in. It was just a matter of time before he slipped up.

"And you have plenty of Time, don't you Ebenezer?"

That voice again!

It couldn't possibly be Scratchitt because he was already half way across the board room. It was amazing someone his size could move that fast.

"Wait a minute Scratchitt."

Scratchitt froze. His hand gripped the brass door handle so tightly that Scrooge could see the fleshy knuckles turn white. Scrooge could hear his heavy breathing from across the room.

"Did you just say something?"

Bob Cratchitt froze, his brain just refusing to react. What did the man want from him? Surely he wasn't going to change his mind? Or perhaps he hadn't, perhaps he had never intended to give him the extra week in the first place. Even worse, it was some kind of test he had to pass before he could escape with the precious gift of seven days that would never come again but would remain with him and Ellen forever. Why couldn't he think? The clock was ticking so loudly he couldn't concentrate. Soon it would be Christmas Day. Of course! Christmas! A rabbit set free from a snare could not have felt more relief. He turned towards Scrooge his face beaming.

"Merry Christmas Sir, Merry Christmas and a Happy New Year!"

The man was obviously some way short of a full cellar. Merry Christmas! His kid was sick, he'd just lost a week's holiday and the imbecile stood there grinning like he was auditioning for the part of Quasimodo. There were certainly bells ringing in this guy's head. H.R. had probably employed him to keep the Politically Correct Lobby sweet. What a sad world we live in!

"Just get out and shut the door behind you Scratchitt."

The smile died prematurely on Cratchitt's lips. Wordlessly he complied meekly with his employers' command. The door creaked as it shut tight like a coffin lid in an ancient Gothic vault. A coffin lid! Get a grip. The evening's events were forcing Scrooge to face an uncomfortable reality. He had been working too hard and this was obviously his body's way of forcing him to confront the situation. His nerves were a little frayed was all. He sat down heavily on one of the padded walnut chairs studiously avoiding the one that appeared to have a damp patch spread across its surface like a dark stain.

A drink! Another drink! Two in one night, this was becoming a habit. If he wasn't careful he'd end up like Valarie. He pushed the thought away like an unwelcome guest. He would not go there. Valarie was the past, the distant past and that is where she would stay. His eyes turned towards the window. Outside a an electric firmament of lights lit the darkness where an endless supply of Valarie's were readily available to a man of Scrooge's wealth and power without the suffocating downside of attachment and commitment.

Preoccupied by his thoughts Scrooge could not recall actually crossing the boardroom floor to the drinks cabinet. He stood for a moment blinking in disbelief. There was the bottle of Scotch he had opened and propped against it was a white envelope. It had definitely not been there before, or had it?

He eyed the envelope suspiciously, debating whether to summon Miss Perry and ask her to open it, in these precarious times one could not be too careful. The envelope bore his name, not 'Ebenezer' or 'Mr. Scrooge' or even 'Clinton', a name it was universally understood he detested, but simply 'Benny'. No one had called him that in years. It was a name that only one other person knew because it was she had bestowed it affectionately upon him. It could only be one other, his sister Leah.

This was a place he did not want to go. Even after all these years the memories were still too raw and painful. It was she who had sought him out through half the orphanages in the State. It was to her he had revealed his shameful secret and she who had begun the healing process. When Valarie left him it was to Leah she had turned and Leah had betrayed him. She took Valarie in, took her part against him and in so doing severed the bond between them. Leah's act was not merely a betrayal, it was something much more, a judgment. Surely she of all people understood the reason why the course he had taken was the best for everyone, including Valarie.

His fingers were drawn to the black ink on the white parchment. Slowly they traced the neatly written letters in silent rebellion to their master's command. Helpless as a child confronted with a brightly wrapped gift he tore open the envelope and let it flutter like a dead leaf to the floor. As he unfolded the cheap writing paper he noticed his hands were trembling. This was ridiculous. Even Jacob's foul specter had not unnerved him as much as this ragged piece of paper, but Jacob's words had not the power to wound as did those he now held in his hands. For a moment he was tempted to crumple the letter into a ball and cast it aside as he had done metaphorically many times before. Miss Perry had been well schooled and instructed on what mail was never to reach his personal in-tray. Which raised another question, how had it gotten past Eva in the first place? Christmas was no excuse for a lack of vigilance.

That could wait. He forced his eyes towards the first line and the salutation hooked him as surely as a skilled fisherman snares a trout.

Dearest Benny,

It has been a long time since I heard from you. Too long. Perhaps one day you can find time to reply to one of my letters. So much has happened. But I want you to know that Valarie is well and the baby is doing just fine. A little boy just like her with a full head of auburn hair. She has put the past behind her and wishes you well...

Leah would never know the pain her words inflicted. Had she done so she would never have written them. The implication was clear, Valarie had chosen to conceal the real reason behind her 'miscarriage'. An uncomfortable sensation enveloped him. He could not name it for Guilt had always been excluded from his presence by Expediency and Reason. Yet it was the revelation that Valarie now had a child of her own that made him physically recoil as if struck a blow that rendered him defenseless.

....Not all my news is as cheerful. Stephen left three weeks ago and I

haven't heard from him. It's been four months since he came home. He is so changed Benny. It's not the physical changes the blast inflicted on him, although God knows they are bad enough, it's as if the old Stephen died and a stranger came back in his body...

Stephen? He vaguely remembered a blonde haired child with twinkling eyes that made you feel you were looking at his mother. Stephen had enlisted? Obviously he shared his mother's idealistic tendencies. Always wanting to change the world, but the world was a hard place to change. He knew that and now so did Stephen.

....He began to drink heavily and I think he was taking drugs. I tried to talk to him but he got so angry. He frightened me sometimes Benny. Once when we argued he threatened to leave, said he was going to find some of his ex-army buddies living rough in New York City. Now he's gone. I know it's a long shot but I thought he might come looking for you if he got desperate...

"I would have sent him on his way Sir, but he says he knows you."

Grainger's words echoed in his head like distant thunder. The disfigured features, the missing limb, the bright blue eyes that for a moment held his own. Could it be possible? Well it was too late now whatever. Maybe it was for the best. Self pity was a disease and now the source of the infection had been removed from his sister's presence.

....You probably won't even read this letter Benny. Have you ever read any that I've sent you? It's just I'm pretty desperate right now and it is Christmas, you know, when light shone in the darkness and it's really dark where I'm standing now Benny. I could do with a little light.

God Bless,

Leah

What she wanted was something he could not give. . . hope. To offer hope when there was none was the worst form of abuse. Once hope had been his only companion and each new day they waited expectantly for a loving family to deliver him from the endless nightmare of the orphanage. Hope was deceitful and cruel, a false friend, and eventually he shut it out. He crumpled the letter in his hands and tossed it into the bin. It was too late now, too many bridges had been burnt and the rivers were too deep and wide. But it was as if the very act drained him of his strength. He grasped the bottle of Scotch and sat down heavily on the nearest chair.

PART 3: CHRISTMAS EVE - LATER

Christmas Eve: Later

Scrooge awoke to find the bottle of Scotch half empty. By way of compensation something with large boots had taken up residence inside his head. Someone was hammering on the door. He struggled to his feet levering himself up with one hand pressed down on the hard bed. Hard bed! He rubbed his eyes then opened them wide. He must still be asleep. There could be no other explanation. A little boy in grey shabby shorts stared back at him from the mirror on the tiny dressing table. Behind him the faded rose patterned wall paper he detested with a passion formed a gaudy background to his small frame.

The door opened. Miss Stryker stood looking at him as though she had just discovered a stain on her starched white blouse.

"Dinner is in ten minutes. Be there or the dog gets it. If I had my way he already would have."

Scrooge felt himself stare back defiantly through the child's eyes. All those years had passed and she was long since cold in her grave but still her memory invoked bitterness he could taste fresh on his tongue.

"You're a wicked boy Ebenezer. Those terrible lies you told about Mr. Izzard."

The boy remained silent staring down at the floor. Scrooge yearned to scream his denial at her, to affirm the truth she denied but he was merely a guest. Although physically a helpless spectator his emotions were one with the child he had left so far behind.

"You will be pleased to know that all charges have been dropped. Mr.

Izzard will be back with us in the New Year. We should all be thankful the damage you inflicted was not more permanent."

In response to her words his stomach cramped violently and he almost gagged as he felt the acid sting of bile at the back of his throat. How could he have forgotten what it felt like? Something wet struck his hand and he realized they were tears. His tears. "Were you thinking of going somewhere Ebenezer?"

She inclined her head in the direction of his feet and for the first time he noticed the small battered brown suitcase lying by his bed.

"You'll need a coat."

She plucked his jacket from the chair that stood by the dressing table and tossed it carelessly onto the bed.

"It's started snowing."

He looked out the window. Fresh glistening flakes of snow drifted past the grey tenement blocks only to be trodden underfoot by the restless flow of humanity that daily passed him by. Did he bury his head in his hands or was it the child? Both wept silent tears that flowed from a well-spring deeper than despair. The door slammed shut.

It seemed an eternity he remained sat on the bed his head buried in his hands. He was reminded of the story of Ulysses who ordered himself bound to the mast so he could hear the cries of the Harpies that drove men to their doom. Whatever Power was at work it had bound him with invisible bonds to the body and mind of this helpless child. His body shook as the boy sobbed himself to sleep and the blessed relief of oblivion.

Scrooge awoke suddenly. Someone was outside the door again, knocking gently. He swung his feet off the bed and half stumbled against a large holdall that lay by the side of the bed. What had become of the battered old suitcase? Perhaps they had packed all his belongings while he slept and were now intending to throw him out. Where would he go?

The knocking continued persistently and he heard a voice, soft and gentle. He regained his balance by gripping the dressing table and in that moment gazed into the mirror. The child was gone. Staring back at him suspiciously was the thin, drawn face of a young man who reminded Scrooge of an animal that had been badly treated and now regarded the world and everything in it with an equal measure of mistrust.

"Benny, Benny, it's me, Leah. Please open the door."

"Come in. It's never locked."

He heard himself speak yet it was not his voice just an echo from the distant past.

"Benny, what's wrong? You haven't changed your mind?"

With difficulty he turned away from the young man in the mirror knowing he would never see his face again.

"No, of course not. I just thought you might not come."

He watched the tears well in her eyes and noticed how the sunshine reddened her hair like a wounded halo. She rushed forward and embraced him. He did not resist but he could not respond. The smell of her perfume was still precious to him it spoke of the warmth he had never known until then.

"Do you think I'd let you go after finding you at last Benny?"

She took him by the hand and led him out of the room closing the door quietly on his lost childhood.

Even then he could not believe his deliverance was at hand. Izzard or Stryker would at any moment appear like vengeful angels and bar the way but they never did. As they walked down the grey stone steps towards the waiting limousine Leah slipped her arm inside his and he did not look back. He sunk into the plush upholstery and closed his eyes as the door slammed shut and the car moved away down the darkening street. From the window the shadow of the child he once had been watched helplessly as the young man he had become passed out of view without looking back.

Something had been 'lost' that even Leah could not find. Although they were happy years spent with Leah's adoptive father they were never enough to fill the void that had opened up inside him. Doug had treated him as though he were his own but there are bonds that can only be forged early in life when the spirit is pliable and open and uncontaminated by the world. Still there were times he remembered that were good, when happiness seemed almost within his grasp. The motion of the car and Leah's soothing presence lulled him to sleep.

"Get over there man before someone else beats you to it. Truth is if I were 30 years younger…"

Doug was standing over him grinning like a Cheshire cat the way he always did when he'd drunk a little too much.

"Go on what are you waiting for?"

It wasn't Doug, it couldn't be. Doug died from a massive stroke a long time ago. Memories surfaced their way unbidden to his captive consciousness and he knew with dread certainty where he was. Imprisoned in the body of his former self he found himself rising to his feet. He knew instinctively where he was going just as surely as the doomed moth senses the heat of the flame but is powerless to resist. He wanted to turn and run but felt instead the unfamiliar constriction of his facial muscles as they formed a spontaneous smile. If only he could force his eyes shut. Surely this nightmare must end soon.

She was standing with her back to him wearing the red silk dress that revealed her milk white skin over which auburn hair glistened like fresh leaves in the fall. Leah saw him and motioned him to join them. It was only then that Valarie turned towards him and smiled a smile that still haunted him down a lifetime of sleepless nights. He had almost forgotten just how breathtakingly beautiful she was. At that moment he would have given anything for the power to turn and walk away.

"Benny this is my very best friend Valarie, she's been dying to meet you."

Valarie blushed in response but made no attempt at denial. They gazed at each other without speaking. Two lovers clutching tickets for a first class berth on the Titanic. Why did they have to meet then? The timing was all wrong. Doug had managed to secure him a position in the Company and he was determined to be a success. Relationships were a diversion; they could wait until he was financially secure and invulnerable. He would never be that little boy again alone and dreading the dark. She was smiling up at him. His collar felt unusually tight. The room began to spin and instinctively he shut his eyes.

"Benny are you alright? Did you hear what I said?"

He was no longer standing. Had he fainted and made a fool of himself? Valarie was leaning forward across the table holding his hand, a look of concern on her face. She was no longer wearing the red silk but a plain Camille crochet grey dress that showed off her great legs. It was the last time she had ever worn it.

Delmonico's was full but her soft tone cut through the din like an archangels' trumpet. He saw the fear and uncertainty in her eyes as she awaited his response.

"Yes, I heard." Scrooge withdrew his hand.

She flinched then lowered her head submissively preparing herself for the inevitable blow to fall. "It's just not the right time for us. Perhaps in a few years when I've established myself. Babies and business don't mix."

How hollow his words sounded, even then.

"That's the thing with babies Benny, they have their own timetables. What do you suggest, I send it back?"

His silence uttered the words he did not have the courage to speak.

"Oh no, Benny, not that. You can't ask me to do that?" She leaned back in her chair a wounded animal ready to take flight.

"It's for the best Baby, believe me. It's a hard world out there and when we bring a child into it I want to be sure he's going to have the best." He leaned forward to cover her hand but this time she pulled away and stood with such force her chair tumbled backwards onto the floor attracting some attention from adjacent tables.

"Valarie wait!"

But she had taken flight. He left money on the table and followed her out into the night. There was a chill in the air and she had left without her coat. He would find her and bring her home. She would see reason; she always did eventually, for he possessed the power to bend people to his will, especially Valarie. One day she would thank him for it.

Outside Delmonico's Scrooge stood and watched his former self stride purposefully down the crowded side-walk gradually merging into the anonymous throng. He heaved a sigh of relief, grateful to have been released from that particular nightmare.

The distant thunder of angry words reverberated in his head, Accusations, Justifications and Recriminations the Unholy Trinity of a broken world. She had resisted him but at a terrible price.

According to Leah the overdose had not been a cry for help, but a desperate attempt to be heard above the yelling and screaming that had become their life. She miscarried. He simply carried on. What else could he do? They separated soon after and he had heard nothing from her since. Until tonight that was. Now she had the child she craved and he...

"Your chariot awaits Ebenezer."

The words splashed against his face like icy water. He turned around half expecting to see Jacob standing in the shadows. A yellow taxi cab was parked alongside him it's passenger door wide open. He didn't recall summoning one but wasn't going to look a gift horse in the mouth. Not tonight anyway. He clambered in and shut the door firmly as if in so doing he could finally exorcise the images from his past.

"Take me to the Interstellar Building."

He was totally unprepared for what happened next. This was how those astronauts must feel when the shuttle surges off the launch pad and the G-force compresses their bodies back into the seat. A kaleidoscope of coloured light flowed past the window as powerful as an electric river in flood.

"For God's sake man, what are you trying to do kill us?"

"You don't escape that easily Dude."

It took a monumental effort but Scrooge managed to turn his head enough to catch site of the driver. He was clad in a black leather biker's jacket, his face totally obscured by a helmet with a tinted visor. With difficulty Scrooge ignored the presumptuous informality.

"Where are you taking me?"

Whatever it was it could not possibly be worse than the horrors he had already endured.

"A party Dude. We all know how you love parties?"

The voice, distorted by the visor, made Scrooge feel he had been suddenly transported into the middle of a science fiction movie. Only this character came equipped with a heavy dose of sarcasm.

The taxi, or whatever this contraption was, had stopped. Scrooge gazed out of the window in a frantic attempt to reorientate himself. The question was not only where was he but *when* was he. The scene outside looked vaguely familiar if you had ever lived in the suburbs. They all looked pretty much the same. He was relieved that he did not recognize this particular street. It seemed ludicrous to think now that he had been grateful to Doug for lending him the money to put a deposit on such a nondescript place. Doug had been like an overgrown puppy who just wanted to please. Scrooge remembered how fond he had been of Valarie, of them both. It was just as well Doug had not been around for the split and its consequent fall out. He resolved to remain in his seat whatever happened.

The door was unceremoniously yanked open.

"Out!"

There was no denying this imperious command. Scrooge got out.

Instead of standing on the side-walk he found himself inside the house that they had just parked alongside. Through the window he could see the yellow taxi with the door wide open. The Thing with the motorcycle helmet stood alongside him its head tilted in the direction of a bed situated in the centre of the room upon which a small child of about three or four years lay motionless. He was not asleep for his eyes were open and fixed intently upon Scrooge.

"He can see me."

The thought disturbed him profoundly but he could not say why.

"You and I are invisible to mortal eyes. Yet," the creature weighed its words carefully, "young children often possess the power to sometimes pierce the veil and gaze into our realm for they are as yet uncorrupted by the world."

If that little speech was meant to offer reassurance to Scrooge it had the opposite effect. References to 'veil' and 'realm' did nothing to quell the turbulent waves of panic crashing against his skull.

The child lowered his eyes as though the effort of keeping them open had drained him of strength. It was only then that Scrooge noticed the I.V. line inserted in the child's arm.

"What's wrong with him?"

His companion did not answer and at that moment a woman entered the room carrying a glass of water. She sat by the bed and handed the child the drink. Even the act of smiling appeared an effort and he sipped the drink without speaking.

"Daddy shouldn't be long now. Try and get some sleep. You know who's coming tonight."

The child closed his eyes but whether this was in response to his mother's prompting or the inevitable consequence of his weakened state Scrooge couldn't tell. The mother watched the child for a moment before leaning over and kissing him on the cheek. The front door slammed and she raised her head. Into the room rushed a figure still clad in his snow dusted coat. She rose and placed a finger on her lips. The man looked crestfallen.

"I was hoping to get back before he went to sleep."

He looked vaguely familiar and suddenly recognition dawned upon Scrooge.

Scratchitt! The guy who'd tried to pull a fast one with the holidays earlier. Why were they in Scratchitt's house?

"What kept you?" There was a hint of mild admonition in her voice. "Or should I say who kept you?"

Scratchitt shifted uneasily on his feet and Scrooge noticed he did not look at his wife when he answered.

"He's a busy guy Ellen. Running a huge corporation and everything. He saw me eventually."

"Yeah he's a regular guy all right. Why do you always do that Bob?" She glanced at the child conscious that she had raised her voice. He did not stir. Seizing the moment her husband stepped forward and embraced her in a bear like hug. She stiffened at first then her face broke into a smile that seemed to light up the room.

"I've got the extra week."

In response to what Scrooge felt was hardly news of global significance his wife whooped with delight.

"Well God Bless Mr. Scrooge!"

He had definitely missed something. Together they sat down by the side of the bed.

Scrooge noted he had failed to mention the two weeks he would lose in the summer.

"He's H.I.V. Positive"

Scrooge jumped. He had almost forgotten the Creature was there. Something about the scene before him held a fascination he could not explain.

"You mean Aids?"

Instinctively he took a step backwards. Had he shaken hands with the guy earlier? He was almost certain he hadn't, almost.

"You have nothing to fear from this child Ebenezer."

Embarrassment flushed Scrooge's cheeks.

"How long has he got?"

"Not long. This may be his last Christmas."

"Is there nothing they can do?"

"There are medications that could prolong his life for many years but they are expensive and beyond the means of this family."

"Even if they could I suppose it would only delay the inevitable."

"If that were true Ebenezer I would not be here."

The creature turned towards him and though he could not see its face he felt the intensity of its scrutiny burn deep.

"Are you telling me the child can be cured?" Scrooge knew that was impossible the cynicism in his voice betraying his lack of faith.

"When you love Ebenezer, every second is precious, every minute, every hour, every day, and every year. Love keeps its own Time. Have you never loved Ebenezer?"

It was a question he could, or would not answer. Not now, not ever. Instead he did what he did best and took the offensive.

"That must have been tough?"

"Tough?" It worked, the creature sounded confused.

"Well, you know, adopting a kid only to find it has Aids."

There followed a silence and Scrooge could not conceal the sense of satisfaction he always felt when his words found their mark.

"Ah! I had forgotten how much store you earthbound creatures place on creed and color. You misunderstand Ebenezer. They chose the child because of his affliction."

"They chose a kid because he had Aids?"

If this had been a boxing match Scrooge had just been hit with a sucker punch.

"Do you now understand what you have missed? They chose to love even though they knew it would be the source of great pain as well as great joy. That is the most precious kind of love Ebenezer. Come, my hour is nearly done."

He was reluctant to leave but the creature gave him no choice. It seized Scrooge by the arm and led him to the door. Scrooge glanced back quickly over his shoulder at the child on the bed. This time the child did not open its eyes and Scrooge experienced a tug of disappointment. They stepped into the hallway where a modest Christmas tree sparkled and glittered, joyfully defiant of the dark. The creature opened the front door and Scrooge was propelled out into the street.

PART 4: THE CONCLUSION

He stumbled striking his knees on the side-walk. The taxi was waiting but he was no longer outside Scratchitt's house. He stood and gazed upwards. The Interstellar Inc Building reached into the night sky as though grasping at the cold indifferent stars, bathing him in its monstrous shadow.

"See Ebenezer, you have built your tower toward the heavens but what name have you made for yourself?"

The creature moved towards the taxi and Scrooge made to follow but it held up a gloved hand.

"Farewell Ebenezer. Someone waits for you."

Scrooge recalled a line of verse:

"Like one who on a lonesome road doth walk in fear and dread,

And having once turned round walks on, and no more turns his head,

Because he knows a frightful fiend doth close behind him tread."

And immediately wished he hadn't. He watched the taxi until it was swallowed up by the hollow dark streets not because of any sentimental attachment to his late companion but because like the man on that lonesome road he also did not wish to turn round.

This was nonsensical. Whatever had happened to him tonight this was still New York City and he was still one of its most powerful denizens. There was nothing he need fear. Nothing! Yet he was afraid. Worse, he was vulnerable. Emotions buried long ago stirred deep within breaking through the dead ground like fresh shoots in a barren field.

"Someone waits for you."

He sensed its presence behind him and with grim determination he turned to face whatever being had passed through the eternal veil into the world of men.

A little girl with auburn hair stood at the top of the steps looking down at him. She was dressed in the pink party dress he recalled her wearing earlier that evening. Their eyes met briefly then she turned and walked towards the building until she vanished from sight. Overwhelmed by a sudden and irresistible need to confront the child he raced up the steps.

At the top he paused to regain his breath and make a mental note to have serious words with his personal fitness coach. There was no sign of the girl with auburn hair. There was no sign of anyone. Security was conspicuous by their absence. He moved cautiously towards the entrance as though approaching an alien edifice of unknown origin. A portal to strange new worlds where he was unsure he would be welcomed with open arms.

The foyer was deserted. Only the Christmas tree festooned with a myriad twinkling lights lit the gloom like distant constellations. Scrooge needed no light. He knew the way. She had shown him earlier. When he got to the lift it was already in use as he knew it would be. He watched its progress upwards until it stopped at the floor that housed his private hospitality suite where many lucrative deals had been struck with some of the world's most influential and powerful individuals. It should not have been possible for the child to have accessed this level, but this was no ordinary child. This was no ordinary night. He waited for the lift to descend. When it did he stepped inside.

It was empty. The doors closed and he ascended. It stopped where he knew it would and the doors slid apart. The hallway was also empty. There was no sign of the child. He debated whether he should return to the level below where normality beckoned but in truth the decision had already been taken by a far Senior Executive and no alternative option was open to him. He stepped out into the hallway and walked slowly towards the Hospitality Suite.

The suite was in use. Someone from Security stood sentinel outside the door, his massive arms folded in the classic universal pose that marked their breed. Scrooge's brow furrowed, he had given no authorization for its use. Perhaps now the orchestrator of this bizarre conspiracy would at last reveal himself. Scrooge yet clung to the forlorn hope that the evening had been somehow ingeniously contrived by an as yet person or persons unknown. Anger, born of the humiliating experiences he had been forced to endure this dreadful evening, surged through his body and he seized the handle of the door with aggressive intent. Immediately massive fingers closed around his wrist with such force pins and needles pierced his hand and he began to lose feeling in his arm.

"Your invite please Sir."

The impassive voice exuded authority that Scrooge calculated no force on earth could deny. The Sentinel motioned towards Scrooges' jacket at the same time releasing his grip. Scrooge rubbed his hand ruefully but discretion advised him not to make any further issue of the matter. Instead he submissively reached inside his jacket and felt the hard corner of a card that he was sure had not been there before.

It was gilt edged with two balloons in the left hand corner, one red and one blue. Written upon it in a child's hand was just one word, *Papa*. The universe imploded and he felt his very being sucked into a dark swirling vortex from which there would be no way back. He leaned against the wall to steady himself and felt the invitation plucked from his hand.

"This seems in order Sir. You may enter."

The door opened and Scrooge stepped into the vortex. The hospitality suite was a large room admittedly but the scene before him defied logic. He recalled a time in the orphanage when Miss Stryker had left her hand mirror on his dressing table. He had picked it up and turned it towards the mirror so that the images seemingly repeated themselves endlessly into infinity. How he had longed to be able to step into one of those alternative universes but it was merely an illusion and fate bound him irrevocably to the reality that remained.

Before him the room stretched away impossibly towards a lost horizon. In its centre around a table adorned with countless balloons were seated a host of children as numerous as the distant stars. Their faces, illuminated by an inner light, were turned towards him as if his arrival had been long anticipated. He stood transfixed as they continued to stare at him radiant with an innocence untainted by the world. It was like looking into the sun and he tried desperately to avert his eyes but he was held by their unwavering gaze that pierced to the very root of his being laying him bare before them. There was no condemnation in their expression, only compassion, yet he was filled with a nameless fear and dread as must a condemned man who faces his executioner and the final judgment beyond.

As though part of one single entity the children turned away and the moment passed. For the first time Scrooge noticed that sat next to each child was an adult wearing an expression of mingled wonder and awe similar, he realized, to the one he probably now wore. A small hand slipped into his own. The child with auburn hair stood before him.

"I'm glad you came Papa."

It was a name he had heard many times but never before directed at him. Valarie had always referred to her late her father as Papa. Scrooge had never known him. He died shortly before he and Valarie had first met but she spoke of him often with a fondness that Scrooge found irritating and which aroused within him an emotion he refused to acknowledge. Why should he be jealous of any man? Especially someone who no longer existed. Yet it was this very fact that irked him. Death had placed him beyond Scrooge's reach and from beyond the grave he had presided over their marriage like a cheap plaster saint. Every perceived indiscretion was sufficient for Valarie to invoke his presence and inevitably Scrooge would fall far short of the exalted standards he had set. Any attempt to discredit his memory only intensified the aura surrounding it. Was it possible that this child...

"Who are you?"

He tried in vain to keep his voice steady. The touch of her hand was unbearably distracting. Something was stirring deep within him, something he had locked away a lifetime ago and banished from his consciousness. Now it had been summoned forth by a child's fragile touch.

"Oh Papa."

She laughed as a child does when teased. Tugging gently at Scrooge she led him to the head of the table where two vacant chairs awaited them. He sat down unable to avert his eyes from her face. Her face, for the second time this night he looked upon the face he had never stopped loving. Her blue eyes held his own and a sudden cold wind embraced his body. Valarie's eyes were green.

"Valarie?"

"I'm not Valarie silly, Valarie is Mama's name."

"Then who are you?"

But even as he spoke the words he knew the answer for it was branded upon his forehead like the mark of Cain.

"Can't you guess?"

"Megan?"

Megan. It was the name Valarie had chosen in deference to her Welsh ancestry of which she was inordinately proud. For once he let her have her way. What did it matter anyway, the child would never be born. It had proved a serious error of judgment for the very act of naming the child bestowed on Valarie a moral strength he never imagined she possessed. Thereafter she resisted him at every turn but the effort drained her vitality and she took refuge in drink. The miscarriage had been a fortuitous consequence.

"That's impossible. Valarie lost our child."

Even now he refused to speak her name. Even now he refused to accept his portion of blame.

"Nothing that has ever lived is truly lost Papa."

She looked at him and the revelation of what he had lost swept over him, a chill wind announcing the onset of a long and bitter winter. Images of what might have been flashed through his mind and he tried to grasp hold of them but they evaded him like autumn leaves scattered in a sudden storm. He bowed his head unable to look at her, unable to look his Megan in the face. A hand touched his cheek brushing away a solitary bemused tear lost on the unfamiliar terrain.

"Why me? Why not your mother? She grieved a long time."

"I know. But Mama doesn't need to see me; she always keeps me close here."

Megan placed a hand across her chest.

"What do you want from me?"

He was ready now, ready to pay any price to end his torment but Megan did not answer.

" What do you want me to do Megan?"

"Set him free Papa."

"Who? Set who free? I don't understand!"

It was he who needed release. His head spun. The still waters of his subconscious had been disturbed and raw emotion clouded his thoughts.

"You must come with me Papa."

Megan stood and taking him firmly by the hand led him towards the door. He turned back for one last look but although the table still stretched toward an unknown destination no one was seated there. The guests had silently departed.

"Who was the party for?" He asked as he embraced the scene one last time.

"It was mine Papa."

He turned sharply in response to Megan's voice which had suddenly deepened and mellowed.

A young woman stood before him. A beautiful young woman with auburn hair and blue eyes.

Eyes that regarded him with a sorrowful solemnity.

"I would have been eighteen today."

He recoiled from the import of her words, at the sudden revelation of all that might have been.

"Christmas Eve. Megan I am so very sorry."

"Papa listen!"

He was stilled before the urgency and authority of her voice and bearing.

"You have no need to be sad for me, but for you there is so little time. Come."

She led him out into the hallway. The Sentinel was no longer at his post. He struggled to keep pace with her and when at last she stopped he took time to catch his breath.

"You must go in alone."

They were outside the Presentation Suite where many deals had been concluded to Scrooge's satisfaction.

"Will I see you again?"

The thought of losing her once more was almost too much to bear.

"That is no longer my choice."

His heart lifted as he realized she too felt pain at the prospect of parting.

"Papa go!"

The urgency in her voice compelled him to action.

The heavy paneled door towered ominously above him and he reached forward tentatively as though contact with its polished surface were an act of hostile intent. He paused and turned to her one last time seeking reassurance and drawing strength from her presence but she was gone. Driven by a grim resolve he opened the door and entered.

Darkness enfolded him deeper than the night. Where were the lights? The lights were programmed to activate as soon as someone entered the room. He frantically struggled to compose himself but the events of the night were persistent intruders disrupting his attempts to think logically. Gradually he formed an image in his mind of the suite's layout. The central sector of the room was arranged like a mini cinema but instead of a single screen a multitude of large monitors had been assembled giving the appearance of one immense screen. Each monitor represented a different satellite channel owned and controlled by Interstellar Inc. It was a persuasive tool in the hands of a master manipulator. Once a prospective client realized just how much influence and control could be exerted through these portals they were practically begging to be allowed to conclude a deal on whatever terms he cared to propose.

He had just about fumbled his way to the seats without causing himself any damage when the screens activated spontaneously and the darkness reluctantly slunk back into the shadows gathering in black pools around the room's perimeter. Scrooge found the nearest chair and sat down heavily his heart pounding hard against his chest.

"Ebenezer Scrooge, you have been weighed in the scales and found wanting."

Scrooge sprang to his feet. The voice had come from behind. He was obviously not alone. Was there someone seated in the back row or was it merely a manifestation of his feverishly overburdened imagination?

"Who's there? What do you want?

He peered intently into the gloom but the shadows flickered and shifted deceptively as an image on the screen began to grow and take shape.

"Interstellar Incorporated International regret to announce the death of their CEO and distinguished leader Ebenezer Clinton Scrooge III following a brief illness."

Scrooge spun round facing the screen and stepped forward drawn like a moth to it's shimmering brightness. Looming over him was the figure of Ed Burgh, the networks' premier anchor man. Each monitor displayed a different part of Ed's anatomy like some gigantic digital jigsaw assembled for this single purpose. Impossibly white teeth flashed briefly as he spoke in appropriately low somber tones.

" Although head of arguably the most powerful and influential media empire on the planet Ebenezer Scrooge ironically shied away from the glare of publicity. Such was his passion for privacy that he famously refused an interview with Forbes magazine and was rarely to be seen in public. It is rumored that after the late Princess Diana his was the most prized scalp coveted by the now infamous paparazzi."

What the hell was this guy talking about? One thing for sure, after next week the only news he would be able to deliver would be from the front page of the *Spare Change News* on some street corner down-town.

"Although he mingled with presidents, world leaders, captains of industry and even royalty, Scrooge remained an enigma leading to frequent comparisons with Howard Hughes, probably the most famous recluse of modern times.

He was named Ebenezer as apparent acknowledgement of his Jewish roots. His father survived the horrors of Dachau although it is believed many of his family perished...."

Just like the Cheshire Cat, Ed Burgh disappeared without warning and was replaced with an older grimmer image that Scrooge recognized immediately. He stared at the black and white grainy footage that he knew so well. Footage he had privately viewed many times before. It had become a constant source of strength. Whenever difficult decisions needed to be taken in his personal or business life he would turn to it and draw deeply from its bitter waters which never failed to refresh his spirit and harden his resolve. Now it loomed before him more terrible than ever.

A queue of people huddled together on a railway siding alongside a row of cattle trucks. Men, women and children carrying an assortment of baggage presided over by soldiers moved slowly towards the open doors of the trucks. Children with bemused expressions looked up at their parents for reassurance. They in turn struggled to suppress the fear and quell the panic mounting within as they offered what little comfort they could. For Scrooge it was akin to watching a Greek tragedy of epic proportions where one knows the fate that awaits the hero but is powerless to intervene and change his destined course.

Yet this image had sustained him and made him strong. Never would a child of his enter this world powerless before the winds of fate or the whims of men. That is what Valarie had failed to comprehend. It was not that he did not want the child; he did not want Megan to ever become a victim of capricious circumstance as so many children had been. As he once was. Looking at the images before him could any man honestly deny that it would have been better if those children had never been born?

Something in the image caught his eye. Something that had not been there before. A sudden surge of anger consumed him. Someone had tampered with his private footage for amongst the many shades of grey he glimpsed a flash of color. It was a child's dress. The child, clutching a teddy bear in her arms, was looking around frantically. She had obviously been separated from her mother in the crowd and its relentless driven march forward. Her dress was pink. Her hair was auburn. She lifted her head and stared directly at him through pleading, frightened eyes her face now filling the screen.

"Megan!"

It could not be. As he watched she was pushed forward. The doors of the cattle truck were open and people were being herded inside without dignity or compassion. Megan was lifted roughly up in the arms of a soldier but before he was able to discard her unceremoniously two bare arms reached out and lifted her gently inside and she disappeared into the shadows. Yet it was not this unexpected act of compassion that caused Scrooge to bow his head and weep as he had not wept since his own barren childhood. In her last moments, even as the soldier held her in his arms she had turned to look directly at him and she was smiling.

The image fragmented and was gone. In its place the somber countenance of Ed Burgh returned.

"Scrooge was born in New York City in February 1960. A new era was dawning for Americans and a mood of optimism swept the country but for Ebenezer Scrooge a far darker destiny dogged the family's footsteps. In October of the following year both his parents were tragically killed in an auto-mobile accident when their car collided head on with a truck whose driver was proved to be heavily under the influence of alcohol.

With no immediate family to care for him the infant Ebenezer Scrooge and his elder sister were placed in care. The infant Scrooge to a state run orphanage.

Here he remained for the next sixteen years. Very little is known about this period of his life as he steadfastly refused to disclose any details. Speculation fuelled by the tabloid press following the investigation, and subsequent convictions, of many employees suspected of child abuse in state institutions cannot be categorically confirmed or denied. What we can say is that Ebenezer Scrooge surmounted enormous personal tragedies and setbacks that would have discouraged most men."

Ed Burghs teeth shimmered like the Northern Lights then vanished. In his place an enormous window appeared viewed from the perspective of the interior of a room gloomy with shadows. Through the window streets lamps lit the twilight briefly illuminating silhouettes of passers by as they hurried to keep pace with their silver breath as it snaked through the chill evening air.

He knew the room as intimately as any prisoner knows each stone of his solitary cell. He had been back there once before this evening and harbored no desire to return. Countless times he had stood at this window and watched as parents with their children passed carelessly by on the other side. Their laughter seemed to beckon to him and in his imagination he would run outside and follow after them. How he yearned to be allowed inside that closed circle called family but they all disappeared into the distance before he could catch up with them, blissfully unaware he even existed.

The window drew closer and Scrooge guessed he was now viewing the room through the occupant's eyes, the boy he had once been an eternity before. Two people were leaving the orphanage, a woman and a man. Which child, he wondered, would even now be experiencing the stinging slap of rejection? What he would not have given to be walking down those steps between them the touch of their hands upon his own; but he was never allowed out of his room when visitors called for he was one of the 'special' children. It was as the man stooped to enter the car that he caught sight of his face. On the screen before him the boy pressed his face longingly against the window pane but Scrooge stepped back, suddenly filled with confusion.

The young man's face had been his own.

He sensed a revelation of great significance was within his grasp but just as you reach out to touch your reflection in a still pool it shattered and was gone. The voice of Ed Burgh once again reverberated inside his head.

"It was this indomitable spirit that enabled him to forge a media empire informed observers believe influenced many of the major political decisions of our generation. But like all great men he was not without his critics. The most strident voices alleged that Interstellar was deployed as a propaganda tool by governments worldwide seeking to gain popular support for policies difficult to justify on moral grounds alone. They commonly cite the devastating humanitarian cost of ensuing global conflicts that such policies allegedly ignited."

A plane screamed overhead and suddenly a group of naked children were running towards Scrooge, terror etched on their faces. Some screamed in pain their bodies blistered and raw. One of the children appeared to be running straight at him her arms outstretched imploringly. It was, he knew, merely an optical illusion yet what compelled him to move towards the screen was the child's face. He recognized her at once and stretched out his arms to offer her refuge.

He swiftly withdrew has hands as a black cloud of flies seemingly disturbed by his sudden movement burst upwards and although he knew it to be merely an image he involuntarily covered his mouth. The very thought of their defiling presence sickened him. The screen cleared and a child with enormous eyes and emaciated body stared up and through him to a place beyond the suffering of this world. It was held in the arms of a skeletal creature he took to be its mother. She watched impassively as the flies returned and settled on the child's face. Neither mother or child attempted to drive them away. He sensed they had both traveled far in search of food and their journey had taken them past despair to that desolate place called Resignation. The image receded and he witnessed as from a great height a ragged queue of humanity lost in the shimmering heat of the desert. He dared not look too closely for he feared that somewhere amongst that abandoned mass of humanity was a child with auburn hair.

The image blurred and was replaced with others. A kaleidoscopic display of horrors that numbed his senses until Scrooge felt he could bear no more. Children with soulless expressions swaggered around with guns instead of toys. Lost boys and girls who had never heard of Neverland. Children filled with hate cast stones at soldiers. By dusty roadsides children begged for bread or sold themselves in filthy brothels.

"Please, enough!"

Scrooge covered his face but he could not block out the noise and the stench that assailed his other senses.

"But great men rise above the petulant criticism of their peers. Never once did Ebenezer Scrooge dignify these base charges with a response. His silence an eloquent testimony that truth will stand on its own merits."

Scrooge groaned. Why didn't the man shut up?

"And you called us monsters."

It could not be. Scrooge spun around. The room was no longer empty. Two figures clothed in shadow stood behind the back row of seats. He did not need to see their faces for he had never been able to completely exorcise the sound of their voices from his head. It was Stryker who spoke.

"You were monsters. We were children. You were supposed to protect us."

"You never went hungry did you Ebenezer?"

"You always had clothes to wear."

"A warm bed to sleep in."

"Not like those children."

Izzard and Stryker spoke in turn. An infernal double act.

"Besides we couldn't have been that bad."

"Else you would have left us long ago."

"What are you talking about? I did leave. "

"Did you Ebenezer? Did you really."

Stryker spoke in the matronly tones she loved to affect when about to discipline one of her charges.

"You're both dead!"

"But not to you Sonny, not to you."

As, once more, Scrooge stood helpless before them they stepped back and were immediately swallowed by the dark.

"Even now tributes to the life and accomplishments of Ebenezer Clinton Scrooge III are flooding in by the hour." Ed Burgh would not be silenced, especially by the dead.

"However, in keeping with his life, the funeral is expected to be a very private affair for close friends and family members only."

Assured that the shades of Izzard and Stryker were no longer lurking in the shadows Scrooge slumped down in the front row and listened to the details of his funeral arrangements. It certainly would be a small gathering. Perhaps he should have taken Face Book more seriously.

Like a shark breaking through surface water the shiny grill of a gleaming black hearse raced towards him. It was the first of a cortège of three that wound their way from Manhattan towards the Mount Hebron Cemetery where the parents he could not remember had been laid to rest half a century before. Their remains were now housed in a private mausoleum and it was here the cortège came to a halt.

The doors opened and he watched with mounting trepidation to see who would emerge.

Grainger, as dependable as a rock, was the first to alight and open the doors of the mourner's car. Leah stepped out shielding her face against the low winter sun. She was followed by another woman whose auburn hair he glimpsed beneath her wide brimmed hat. Valarie had come. He had not expected that and he doubted whether he would have done the same had the roles been reversed. The third occupant was also a woman. He recognized her immediately despite the fact she kept repeatedly dabbing her eyes with a handkerchief apparently overcome by the emotion of the occasion. It was Eva. He was surprised by the way her presence affected him. It was not just gratitude that she had elected to attend but something deeper and more personal.

There were just two occupants of the third.

"Scratchitt!"

What on earth were Scratchitt and his wife doing there? What had he ever done for them? His thoughts fled back to the sick child in the bedroom. The way the wife had responded when told Scratchitt had been given an extended holiday.

"Love keeps its own time Ebenezer."

So he was not alone but he did not care any more, a dam within him was cracking under the remorseless pressure of wasted years bloated with regret and recriminations. He bowed his head but he could not shut out the dark night that enveloped his soul.

"My brother was a solitary man. Not an easy man to know or love, so I thank you all for coming."

Leah's voice drew him back from the void as she had so many years before.

"His had not been an easy life. We lost our parents when Benny was still a child. We grew up apart. I was lucky. A wonderful couple adopted me and made me their own. I assumed the same had happened to Benny. When I eventually decided I wanted to find my brother my parents supported me in every way possible.

He was not living with a loving family as I had always imagined. All the happy carefree years I had spent growing up he had spent in state institutions. He never talked about those years and we never asked. Yet I have always carried a terrible sense of guilt that I did not look for him sooner, perhaps then…"

Leah paused to compose herself. No one stirred.

"No Leah!"

Scrooge was on his feet now and moving towards her image on the screen.

"You saved me!"

But she could not hear him. No one could.

"We brought him home. My parents loved him as they had loved me. Yet…it was as if a part of Benny never really left that dreadful place. I was too late."

Scrooge opened his mouth to protest once more but the words died stillborn on his lips for the truth was taking shape before him more terrible even than the shades of Stryker and Izzard.

"Then he met my dear friend Valarie and I hoped..."Her voice faded as she looked at Valarie who bowed her head in response. Leah did not mention Megan by name but she was there as substantial as the air about them.

"After the divorce Benny changed. He refused to see or speak with me. If it had not been for Eva I would have lost him again. She read the letters he would not open and never failed to reply."

Eva! He should feel angry and betrayed, yet he did not.

"The split between us hurt Stephen badly. He loved his uncle as much as I did. Being a single Mom is not easy and I admit that I felt a sense of relief when he joined the army." She faltered and the silence hung heavy.

"He would have been here today I'm sure if he had known. But I don't know where he is or how to get in touch with him."

She stopped and this time there was no carrying on. Valarie stood and hurried forward to comfort her friend. The service was over. The image blurred and when it refocused they were outside. There was no sign of the others and he noticed that while Leah wore black, Valarie was in grey. Time had obviously passed.

Leah was holding a bunch of roses and they were standing next to some kind of monument but Scrooge was only able to see the base. It bore his name.

Ebenezer Scrooge

"Benny"

1960 – 2010

"Thank you for coming. You have good reason to hate him."

"After losing Megan I hated him more than anything in the world. But hate is so tiring Leah; I just couldn't keep it up forever. Besides although I never knew her I felt so close to Megan. I still do. Then I met Mike and the rest as they say is history."

She glanced at the inscription as though to emphasize the point.

Is that all he had become in the end, a turned page in someone's life?

"But what about you Leah. Still no word from Stephen?"

There was concern in her voice as she drew closer.

"None. It's been over a year now. He left just before Benny died. I wrote to Benny hoping Stephen might come looking for him."

Valarie threw her arms around her friend.

"Don't give up Leah. I almost did but there's always hope. Always."

She turned to the monument in an attempt to distract Leah from her dark thoughts.

"I was kinda surprised by the choice Leah. I thought you might have gone for angels."

"All those years alone in that place he must have felt the world had abandoned him."

Valarie's eyes widened with understanding.

"That's him? That's Ebenezer."

She stood back and Scrooge was given a clear view of the object in question.

A small boy sat on what appeared to be the corner of a bed. He head was turned away to his right. The likeness was uncanny, the pose all too familiar. Scrooge knew exactly where the stone boy would gaze down the long cold years. Not at the hard grey skies but out through an old wooden window suspended in time to the indifferent world that lay beyond.

Leah leaned forward and placed the roses at the feet of the stone child. He noticed that there were dead flowers spread around like a carpet of remembrance. This was not the first time Leah had visited this place.

"I will not forget him again Valarie. Not as long as I have breath in my body. I was too late to save the child and that's why I lost the man.

" She turned to her friend tears flowing freely. "I am so sorry Val that my failure brought you so much pain."

They embraced without speaking. Scrooge watched them walk slowly away arm in arm until he could see them no more. A sudden breeze rustled the dead flowers like a whispered prayer. A petal lifted upwards caught the passing wind and Scrooge reached out impulsively to grasp it. When he opened his hand it was there moist and dark like a scarlet tear.

"No Leah, forget the dead, forget me. Find Stephen. Bring him home."

"But, 'New York is infested with such hopeless individuals seeking solace and oblivion in alcohol or drugs, authors of their own destruction, and as such deserving of no sympathy or special favors.'"

The voice again. Its source, he sensed, stood close behind him and it could read his innermost thoughts. More than this, it had recorded them on some eternal ledger and preserved them as evidence to damn his soul. His thoughts reached out to Leah and Valarie to the hurt he had brought into their lives, was still bringing. And what of the hurt his actions had caused others? He stood guilty as condemned. His punishment would be just. Words recently spoken shed an unexpected light on his troubled spirit;

"There is always hope..." Was it possible, even now?

He resolved to face his accuser and plead forgiveness. For an instant he glimpsed the outline of a commanding figure bathed in a pure light that did not hurt his eyes but obscured his vision. The figure was pointing in the direction of the doors. Scrooge thought he could discern the outline of huge folded wings. The creature moved within a radiant light or maybe light emanated from its very being, he could not tell. One thing was certain, it would countenance no contradiction and Scrooge was bound to obey its gestured command. He moved slowly towards the door with the doleful tread of the condemned and passed beyond.

"Mr. Scrooge, you look absolutely dreadful. Can I get you a drink of water?"

The sight of Eva flapping around him like a startled hen was not the scenario he had anticipated. He nodded meekly giving himself time to compose his thoughts.

Apparently he was in the reception area outside the boardroom and not the ante room to the Afterlife. He stood and walked towards the door rapping it hard with his fist oblivious to the fact that Eva had returned with his glass of water and was now standing open-mouthed behind him.

"See that Eva, real mahogany."

He rapped it again as if confirming his initial diagnosis.

"Yes, real mahogany. It's been like that for as long as I can remember. Are you feeling alright Mr. Scrooge?"

Eva was obviously having difficulty containing her growing sense of alarm.

"What day is it Eva?"

"What day?" He obviously expected a serious answer judging by the earnest expression on his face. She was beginning to become seriously concerned.

"Well in another five minutes it will be Christmas Day."

"Five minutes. Then it's not too late! Sit down Eva we have work to do."

He had to be kidding. Only Scrooge could expect someone to work right up until Christmas Day. He probably spent his spare time squeezing the juice out of prunes.

Why had she stayed with him so long?

It was as if he read her mind.

"Why haven't you gone home yet?"

"I was worried about you."

She was about to qualify the statement but realized she was blushing and scrabbled in her desk for a notepad.

"Yes you have been haven't you?"

His words implied more than was suggested by the immediate circumstances.

Eva shifted uncomfortably and attempted to strike a professional pose.

"Have I ever commented on how attractive you are Eva?"

"Most certainly not!"

He must have been drinking. Or was he simply laughing at her? She had thought he was oblivious to the fact that she was fond of him, well actually, more than fond. Now he was cruelly playing with her affections. She resolved to maintain her composure, do her job and go home. Maybe it was time for a change. New Year, new start.

"I thought so."

There was a note of regret in his voice she found disconcerting.

"Well I should have."

Before she could respond he rapidly changed the subject.

"Eva I want you to write a memo to wire Scratchitt in the New Year."

She remembered the man he had kept waiting for so long.

"You mean Cratchitt, not Scratchitt."

Sounds like the guy was in deep trouble. Only Scrooge would contemplate firing someone on Christmas Eve. Happy New Year Bobby!

"That's him, the one with the sick kid."

Eva shook her head. A sick kid to boot. It just keeps getting better and better.

"Tell him to take the year off, with pay. In fact tell him I'm going to treble his salary."

Eva put down the pen and gave Scrooge a hard stare. This was going too far. If he wanted to mess with people's heads he could do it himself.

"You serious?"

The tone in her voice suggested she had already worked out the answer for herself and it was not one she approved of. Scrooge looked her in the eye and her reservations evaporated. There was something in them she had never seen before, or expected to see ever, compassion and maybe even regret.

"Eva, I have never been more serious in my life. Oh, and find his address for me, I want to pay him a visit in the New Year."

It was becoming more difficult by the second to maintain a professional demeanor.

"Got it."

She kept her response short not wanting him to detect the tremor in her voice.

"Is that all?"

"Not quite."

He paused as though uncertain of what to say next. She never thought she would see the day when Scrooge was lost for words.

"I want you to ring my sister."

"Leah! What, tonight? Don't you realize the time? She'll be asleep. Besides you haven't spoken to her in years"

Scrooge had not realized how close Eva and his sister had become until hearing the protective edge in her voice.

"I'm sorry. That's none of my business."

Scrooge looked at her in a way that suggested he knew it was her business and had been for some considerable time.

"We both know she won't be asleep tonight Eva and we both know why?"

He smiled as a look of consternation crossed her face.

"I read her letter. The one you left by the bottle of Scotch. Guess you know me better than I do myself."

Eva's response was unexpected. She opened the desk drawer and rummaged around frantically but to no avail, the letter was gone.

"It's gone, but how did you know?"

What could he tell her? That some being from the Other Side had been responsible?

She was concerned enough about him already without bringing his sanity into question. He determined to ignore her confusion and press on.

"Just tell her I'm coming for dinner tomorrow and I will have two guests with me."

Eva raised her eyebrows and leaned back in the chair. She eyed him coolly.

"You do realize Christmas dinner is kinda special Mr. Scrooge. She might need a little more notice don't you think?"

"Please call me Benny."

Eva looked like Alice must have when she landed at the bottom of the rabbit hole.

"Benny? Okay! And who shall I say is coming with you…Benny?"

His smile reminded her of a mischievous schoolboy, an analogy she would never have imagined applying to him.

"I would be honored if you would accept my invitation to dinner Eva. Before you object we both know Leah would be delighted to have you."

"You mentioned two guests. Who is the other?"

He noted with satisfaction that she had not refused his invitation merely delayed her acceptance.

"Stephen."

"Stephen? Leah's Stephen! You are kidding me right? Leah doesn't even know where Stephen is."

She scrutinized his face carefully trying to determine whether he was fooling around or genuinely losing the plot

"I know exactly where he is because I saw him earlier tonight. He's here in New York. I didn't recognize him at first. He's changed, and living on the streets hasn't helped."

He held back the part about having him forcibly removed. It was hard coming to terms with being truthful although it felt somehow liberating. Telling the whole truth would be a different ball game completely.

"But if he's living rough how will you find him? It's a pretty big city even with your resources and I don't want to be the one to raise false hopes."

Scrooge ignored the sarcastic undertones.

"I'll find him tonight and he will come home. Make the call please Eva."

She was accustomed to his arrogance. He was used to having his way. It came with the territory of being who he was. But it was not arrogance she saw reflected in his face but a calm unshakeable confidence as if he held a royal flush in five card hand of poker.

"And you expect me to wait around until you get back?"

He turned and smiled at her. It was funny how young he looked when he smiled.

She smiled back. They both knew she had been waiting for him for years.

"Okay, I'll use one of the guest suites."

She watched him cross to the lift where he paused and turned towards her.

"One last thing. The proposed new contract. Memo me to trash it."

Before she could protest and remind him of the inevitable repercussions he had stepped into the lift. He was still smiling as the doors closed.

She dialed the number she knew so well. Leah answered as he said she would.

"Leah it's me...Eva.

No there's nothing wrong, in fact quite the opposite. Leah, you'd better sit down "

Scrooge stood at the top of the steps and gazed out at the city he loved; the city filled this night with countless hopes and fears. A flake of consecrated snow fell from the heavens brushing against his lips. He closed his eyes and in his imagination he was a small boy again, gazing out of a grimy bedroom window to the street below where a young man was about to enter a car parked alongside the orphanage steps. The young man paused, looked up, smiled and beckoned to him. He smiled back and stepped away from the window for the last time. He was going home.

Scrooge opened his eyes. He did not know where Stephen was in the vast teeming metropolis spread before him but it did not matter. A light would guide him; he need only trust and follow. He descended the marble steps into the embrace of the bustling, holy night.

ABOUT THE AUTHOR

Phil Rowlands is a retired head teacher from the Rhondda Valley in South Wales who now devotes himself to his passion for writing. During his teaching career he wrote many plays for children and won several national awards including BAFTAs and prizes at the National Eisteddfod of Wales. He is currently writing a children's novel while collaborating on the creation of a new magazine with a friend who resides in Portland, Oregon. 'A Christmas Carol Revisited' is a tribute to his favorite author Charles Dickens whom Phil regards as not only one of the greatest storytellers who ever lived but a passionate social commentator and reformer.